# Green Light Readers

## For the new reader who's ready to GO!

Amazing adventures await every young child who is eager to read.

**Green Light Readers** encourage children to explore, to imagine, and to grow through books. Created for beginning readers at two levels of skill, these lively illustrated stories have been carefully developed to reinforce reading basics taught at school and to make reading a fun and rewarding experience for children and grown-ups to share outside the classroom.

The grades and ages within each skill level are general guidelines only, and books included in both levels may feature any or all of the bulleted characteristics. When choosing a book for a new reader, remember that every child progresses at his or her own pace—be patient and supportive as the magic of reading takes hold.

## ❶ Buckle up!
### Kindergarten–Grade 1: Developing reading skills, ages 5–7
- Short, simple stories • Fully illustrated • Familiar objects and situations
- Playful rhythms • Spoken language patterns of children
- Rhymes and repeated phrases • Strong link between text and art

## 2 Start the engine!
### Grades 1–2: Reading with help, ages 6–8
- Longer stories, including nonfiction • Short chapters
- Generously illustrated • Less-familiar situations
- More fully developed characters • Creative language, including dialogue
- More subtle link between text and art

*Green Light Readers incorporate characteristics detailed in the Reading Recovery model used by educators to assess the readability of texts through the end of first grade. Guidelines for reading levels for these readers have been developed with assistance from Mary Lou Meerson. An educational consultant, Ms. Meerson has been a classroom teacher, a language arts coordinator, an elementary school principal, and a university professor.*

## Published in collaboration with Harcourt School Publishers

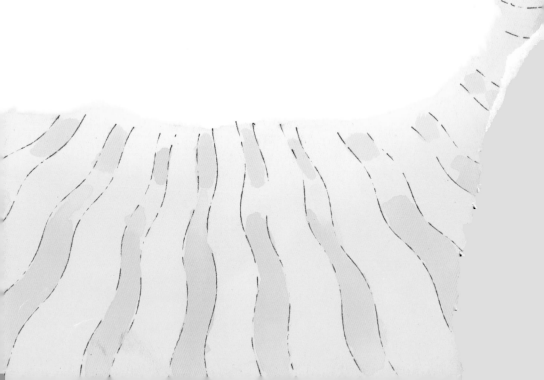

# Cloudy Day
# Sunny Day

# Cloudy Day Sunny Day

## Donald Crews

**Green Light Readers**
**Harcourt, Inc.**
San Diego   New York   London

First Green Light Readers edition 1999
*Green Light Readers* is a registered trademark of Harcourt, Inc.

The Library of Congress has cataloged the original paperback edition as follows:
Crews, Donald.
Cloudy day/sunny day/Donald Crews.
p.   cm.
"Green Light Readers."
Summary: Whether the day is cloudy or sunny, it provides
lots of opportunities for fun and entertainment.
[1. Play—Fiction.  2. Weather—Fiction.]  I. Title.
PZ7.C8862Cl  1999
[E]—dc21    98-3847
ISBN 0-15-201997-9 (pb)

ISBN 0-15-202357-7

B D F H J K I G E C (pb)

A C E G I J H F D B

It's a cloudy day.

A gray day.

A gray and gloomy cloudy day.

A day to stay in and play.

A day for reading books.

A day for make-believe.

A day for drawing and painting.

We have lots of fun on gray, gloomy
cloudy days.

# LOOK! THE SUN! THE SUN!

**THE SUN IS OUT!**

Let's go out.
Let's go out and play.

It's a sunny day.

A running, jumping day.

It's a busy day.

A day to throw and catch.

A day to scream and shout.

A day to fly a kite.

We have lots of fun on busy sunny days.

Cloudy day, sunny day—fun day.

# Meet the Author-Illustrator

*Dear Readers,*

  *On cloudy days, I enjoy reading, writing, drawing, and building model airplanes. On sunny days, I like to take a walk outside and look at everything that is going on around me.*

  *What do you enjoy doing on a cloudy or a sunny day? Enjoy the things you do. Also, find something that you're good at and stick with it.*

*Donald Crews*

# Look for these other Green Light Readers
## in affordably priced paperbacks and hardcovers!

### Level 1/Kindergarten–Grade 1

**Big Brown Bear**
David McPhail

**Down on the Farm**
Rita Lascaro

**Just Clowning Around**
Steven MacDonald
Illustrated by David McPhail

**Popcorn**
Alex Moran
Illustrated by Betsy Everitt

**Six Silly Foxes**
Alex Moran
Illustrated by Keith Baker

**Sometimes**
Keith Baker

**The Tapping Tale**
Judy Giglio
Illustrated by Joe Cepeda

**What Day Is It?**
Patti Trimble
Illustrated by Daniel Moreton

**What I See**
Holly Keller

### Level 2/Grades 1–2

**Animals on the Go**
Jessica Brett
Illustrated by Richard Cowdrey

**A Bed Full of Cats**
Holly Keller

**Catch Me If You Can!**
Bernard Most

**The Chick That Wouldn't Hatch**
Claire Daniel
Illustrated by Lisa Campbell Ernst

**Digger Pig and the Turnip**
Caron Lee Cohen
Illustrated by Christopher Denise

**The Fox and the Stork**
Gerald McDermott

**Get That Pest!**
Erin Douglas
Illustrated by Wong Herbert Lee

**I Wonder**
Tana Hoban

**Shoe Town**
Janet Stevens and Susan Stevens Crummel
Illustrated by Janet Stevens

**The Very Boastful Kangaroo**
Bernard Most

## Green Light Readers
*For the new reader who's ready to GO!*